D1114793

Seriously Silly Stories

ECO-WOLF
and the
THREE PIGS

Compass Point Books
3109 West 50th Street, #115
Minneapolis, MN 55410

Visit Compass Point Books on the Internet at *www.compasspointbooks.com*
or e-mail your request to *custserv@compasspointbooks.com*

Library of Congress Cataloging-in-Publication Data
Anholt, Laurence.
  Eco-Wolf and the three pigs / by Laurence Anholt. Illustrated by Arthur Robins.
    p. cm. — (Seriously silly stories)
Summary: In this modern twist on the classic story of "The Three Little Pigs," Eco-Wolf
and his woodland warriors save the forest and valley from three polluting pigs.
ISBN 0-7565-0630-1 (hardcover)
  [1. Environmental protection—Fiction. 2. Pigs—Fiction. 3. Forest animals—Fiction.
4. Humorous stories.] I. Title. II. Series.
  PZ7.A58635Ec 2004
  [E]—dc22   2003017952

For more information on *Eco-Wolf,* use FactHound
to track down Web sites related to this book.

  1. Go to *www.compasspointbooks.com/facthound*
  2. Type in this book ID: 0756506301
  3. Click on the *Fetch It* button.

Your trusty FactHound will fetch the best Web sites for you!

About the Author
Laurence Anholt is one of the UK's leading authors. From his home in
Dorset, he has produced more than 80 books, which are published all
around the world. His Seriously Silly Stories have won numerous
awards, including the Smarties Gold Award for "Snow White and the
Seven Aliens."

About the Illustrator
Arthur Robins has illustrated more than 50 picture books, all of them
highly successful and popular titles, and is the illustrator for all the
Seriously Silly Stories. His energetic and fun-filled drawings have been
featured in countless magazines, advertisements, and animations. He
lives with his wife and two daughters in Surrey, England.

First published in Great Britain by Orchard Books, 96 Leonard Street, London EC2A 4XD

Text © Laurence Anholt 1999/Illustrations © Arthur Robins 1999

Seriously Silly Stories

ECO-WOLF
and the
THREE PIGS

Written by Laurence Anholt
Illustrated by Arthur Robins

COMPASS POINT BOOKS
Minneapolis, Minnesota

4

In a small tepee in a beautiful valley lived a gentle creature called Eco-Wolf.

There were no cars or houses in the valley, and Eco-Wolf lived at peace with the trees and the wild animals. He spent his time inventing machines that would make electricity from the clear blue river without causing pollution.

One morning, Eco-Wolf was gently explaining to a young animal about litter.

As they spoke, a huge black car roared into the valley. Out climbed three sinister figures dressed in black. The biggest pig stepped forward:

We're the three pigs and we are BAD,
Greedypig, Grabbit and Megadad.

We don't hang about or dilly-dally,
We're gonna build houses in your valley.

So don't get smart, don't no one get funny,
The pigs are out to make some money.

Eco-Wolf couldn't believe what he was hearing.

"Hey, man," he said, "your car is, like, invading my space. You're messing up the valley vibes, piggy brother."

But the pigs only laughed and set to work.

They built a big ugly straw cottage beside the river, with a huge satellite dish on the roof. They had to cut down one or two old oak trees that were in the way, but the pigs didn't care about trees.

As they worked the pigs sang very loudly:

Who's afraid of this eco-guy?
If we messed his hair, he'd be sure to cry.

This valley ain't so peaceful no more,
House number one is made of straw.

We're the three pigs, we don't care a fig,
Megadad, Grabbit, and Greedypig.

12

When they had finished, the pigs put up
a For Sale sign and went inside to eat a
HUGE meal.

Eco-Wolf was very sad to see a house beside the blue river, but he was especially sad about the old oak trees. He called the wild animals to his tepee.

"Hey, wild warrior brother-sisters," said Eco-Wolf. "I don't dig these big pigs. Those trees were kind of like my sister-brothers, too. It makes me huff and puff, man."

So Eco-Wolf and his friends walked up to the door of the straw cottage and rang the bell.

"Big Pig, Big Pig," said Eco-Wolf, "like, let me come in."

"Get outta here, buddy," shouted Megadad, "or you'll get a piggy-punch on your chinny-chin-chin."

Out of the air came all the wild birds of the valley. They carried away every last piece of straw in their beaks, leaving Greedypig, Grabbit, and Megadad with nothing but their TV set.

"That's the last straw. Right, boys?" said
Megadad.

Peace returned to the valley. Eco-Wolf
went back to his Eco-Power machine, and
the clear river flowed.

But the three bad pigs were making
another plan.

"Gather round, boys," said Megadad. "That straw house was a lousy idea. We gotta make somethin' a WHOLE LOT tougher to keep out this Eco-Wolf fella. Right, boys?"

So the bad pigs started work on a wooden house. It had six bedrooms with double-glazed windows, a garage, a swimming pool, and a road leading up to it.

The pigs had to dig up some wild flowers and chase a few rabbits out of their homes, but they didn't care about flowers or rabbits.

While they worked, the three pigs sang even louder:

> So who's afraid of this eco-freak?
> That wolf is just a sneaky geek.
>
> We'll flatten this valley and do it good,
> House number two is made of wood.
>
> We're the three pigs, so good-bye rabbit,
> Greedypig, Megadad, and brother Grabbit.

When they had finished, the three pigs put up a For Sale sign and went inside to eat a COLOSSAL meal.

Eco-Wolf was very sad to see another house in the valley, but he was especially sad about the rabbits. He called the wild animals to his tepee.

"Hey, wild warrior brother-sisters," said
Eco-Wolf, "these big pigs are totally uncool.
Those rabbits were kind of like my sister-
brothers. It makes me huff and puff, man."

So Eco-Wolf and the woodland warriors marched up to the wooden house and rang the bell.

"Big Pig, Big Pig," said Eco-Wolf, "like, let me come in."

"Get outta here, buddy," shouted Megadad, "or you'll get a chop on your chinny-chin-chin."

"Then we'll, like, huff and puff, man, and blow your house into the middle of next week," replied Eco-Wolf.

Out of the fields came all the underground animals of the valley. They dug tunnels deep under the wooden house until it collapsed, leaving the three pigs in a pile of sawdust.

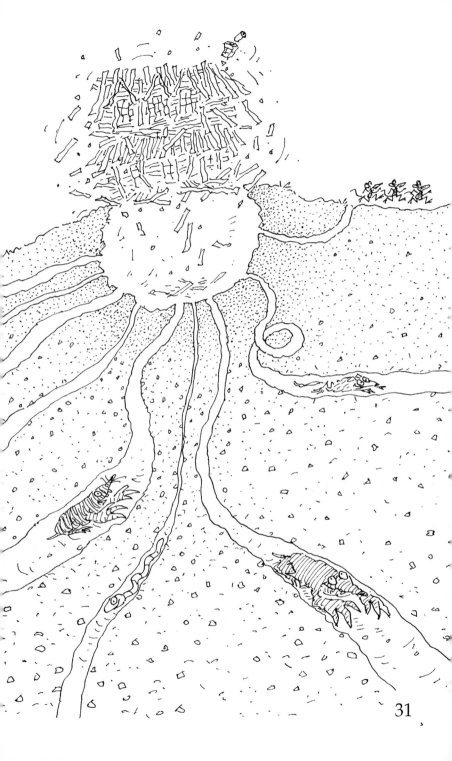

31

Peace returned once more to the valley.
Eco-Wolf went back to his Eco-Power
machine and the blue river flowed.

But the three bad pigs were making an
even bigger plan.

"Gather round, boys. That wooden house was a lousy idea. We gotta make somethin' a WHOLE LOT tougher to keep out this Eco-Wolf guy. Right, boys?"

So the bad pigs started work again. This time they used bricks and concrete. They built a high-rise apartment on top of a multistory shopping mall, with a highway leading up to it.

They needed a lot of electricity, so the three pigs built a huge power station, with a gigantic chimney, right in the middle of the valley.

They had to cut down a forest, and the waste from the power station polluted the river, but the pigs didn't care about forests or rivers.

While they worked, the three pigs sang more loudly than ever:

So who's afraid of this eco-nut?
With his pointy hair
          in his pointy hut.

We'll flatten this valley lickety-quick,
House number three is made of brick.

We're the three pigs, and we are BIG,
Megadad, Grabbit, and Greedypig.

38

When they had finished, the three pigs
put up a For Sale sign and went inside to
eat a MEGA meal.

Eco-Wolf looked at the remains of his beautiful valley. The river was gray, and the air was black and smoky.

"Hey, wild warrior brother-sisters," he said, "this valley was, like, my sister-brother, man. It makes me mad. It makes me ballistic. It makes me HUFF and PUFF, man."

Eco-Wolf and the wild woodland warriors stormed up to the power station. There was a big barbed wire fence all around.

Eco-Wolf pressed the button on the intercom.

"Big Pig, Big Pig," he said, "like, let me come in."

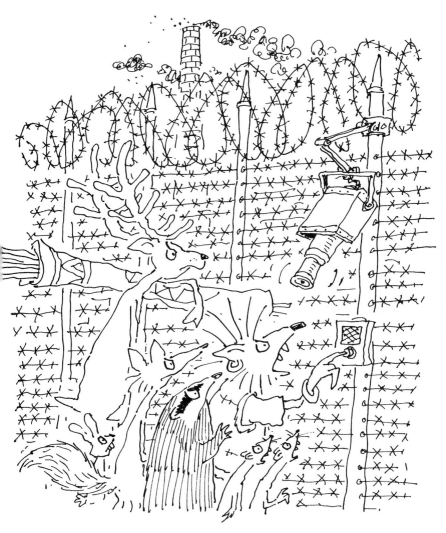

"Clear off, or I'll send out the security guards to give you a knuckle sandwich on your chinny-chin-chin," came Megadad's voice.

"Then I'll, like, huff and puff, man, and blow you and your power station into pork scraps," replied Eco-Wolf.

Deep inside the power station, the three pigs only laughed.

"Hey, wild warriors," said Eco-Wolf, "I'm gonna climb that chimney stack and, like, camp on top, until those big pigs start respecting the planet."

Eco-Wolf strapped his tepee on to his back. The warrior squirrels scrambled up the fence and pulled Eco-Wolf after them. He began to climb the chimney. It was very high, but Eco-Wolf was brave.

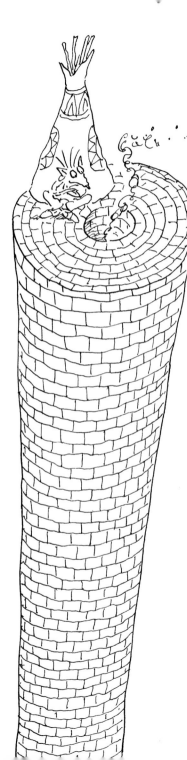

When
he reached
the top, all the
animals cheered.
Eco-Wolf waved once,
unrolled the tepee,
and sat down to wait.

47

"OK, guys. We'll smoke that wolf out," said Megadad. "Right, boys?"

"Right, Dad," replied Greedypig and Grabbit, pulling a lever that turned the station to maximum power.

The heat in the power station started to
build up. Black smoke poured out of the
chimney.

Quick as a flash, Eco-Wolf pulled his tepee over the top of the chimney so that the smoke drifted back down to the three pigs.

"I'll go up and get him, Dad," coughed Greedypig.

He climbed up inside the chimney, but three-quarters of the way up, he got stuck.

"He's too fat," spluttered Grabbit. "I'll go up and get him, Dad."

So Grabbit climbed up inside the chimney, but halfway up, he got stuck, too.

"You're both too fat," shouted Megadad. "I'll go up and get him."

So Megadad climbed up inside the chimney, but only a quarter of the way up, he got stuck, too.

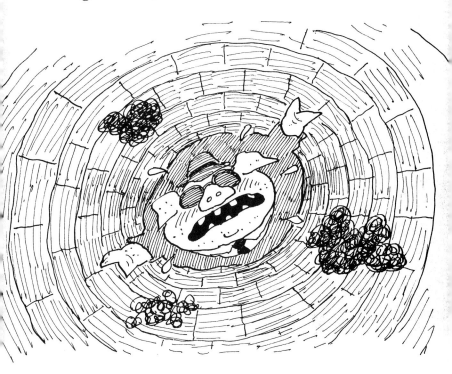

The chimney grew hotter and hotter. The three pigs began to squeal.

Suddenly there was a huge explosion.

Eco-Wolf shot high into the air. Then, holding on to his tepee like a parachute, he drifted gently to the ground. The three bad pigs were fired out of the chimney like piggy cannon balls.

Greedypig landed in the river.

Grabbit landed on the roof of the big black car.

And Megadad smashed right on to
Eco-Wolf's electricity machine.

The high-rise apartment and every one of Megadad's buildings exploded into a thousand tiny pieces.

"Like huff and puff, man. I blew that house down," said Eco-Wolf.

After many days, Eco-Wolf and the woodland warriors finished cleaning up the valley. The three big pigs were made to plant new trees and dig new homes for the rabbits.

While they worked, the three pigs sang
very quietly:

> We're a little bit afraid of this eco-guy
> Who blew our house into the sky.
>
> We'll tidy the valley and do our best,
> To let Mother Nature do the rest.
>
> We're the three pigs and we are sad,
> Grabbit, Greedypig, and Megadad.

When they had finished, the three pigs climbed into their car, drove out of the valley, and far, far away.

At last, the blue river flowed, and the air was clean again. A young animal asked Eco-Wolf how he would make electricity now that his Eco-Water Power machine was broken.

Eco-Wolf smiled. He was already working on a new idea.